To Joseph

To Meet A Dragon

ISBN-13: 978-0692905555

ISBN-10: 0692905553

A&T Publishing

✈Puyallup, Washington

aliveandthankful.com

Lon Cole

I would like to dedicate this book to my nine grandchildren thats two grandsons and seven granddaughters.

There is Joshua, Hannah, Lettie, Isaac, Katherine, Reagan, Ireland, Paisley, and Silver.

What a joy they bring to me and their Grammie. They are truly a gift from above

To Meet A Dragon

Have you ever seen a dragon fly

It's fun to watch them go so high

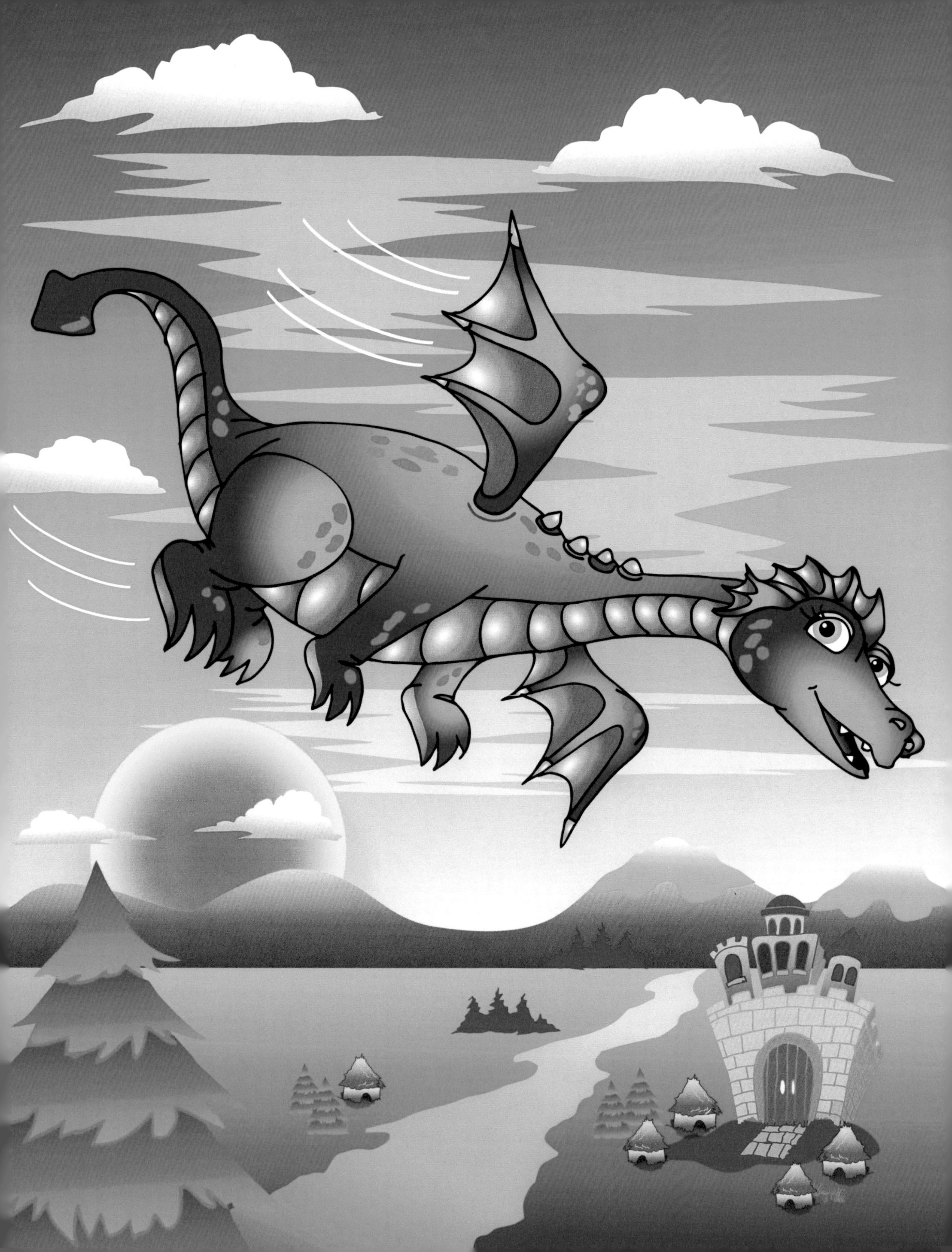

When they sweep down
so fast and low

If you are real close
you'll see them glow

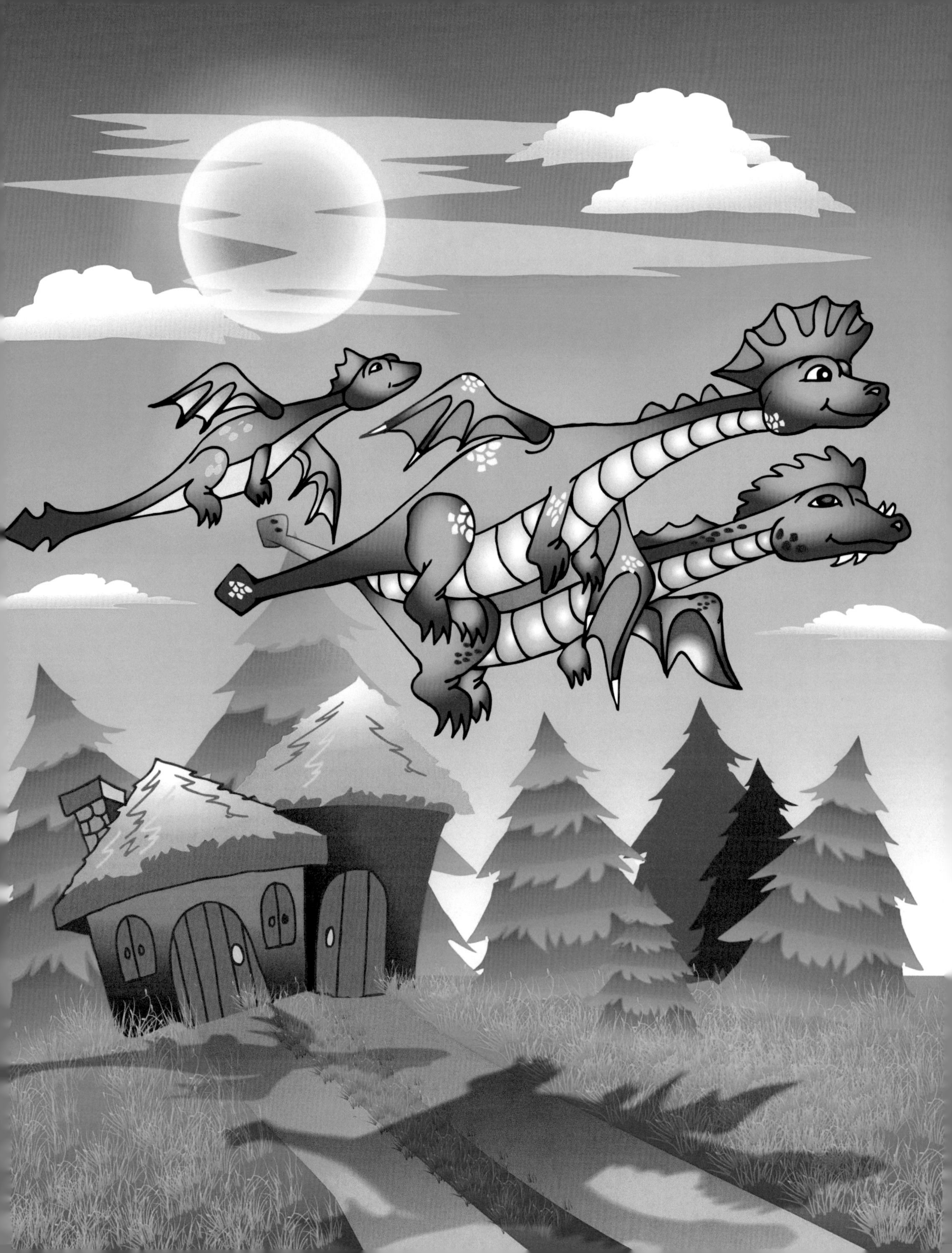

Dragons are as strong as could be

When they make fire
it's awesome to see

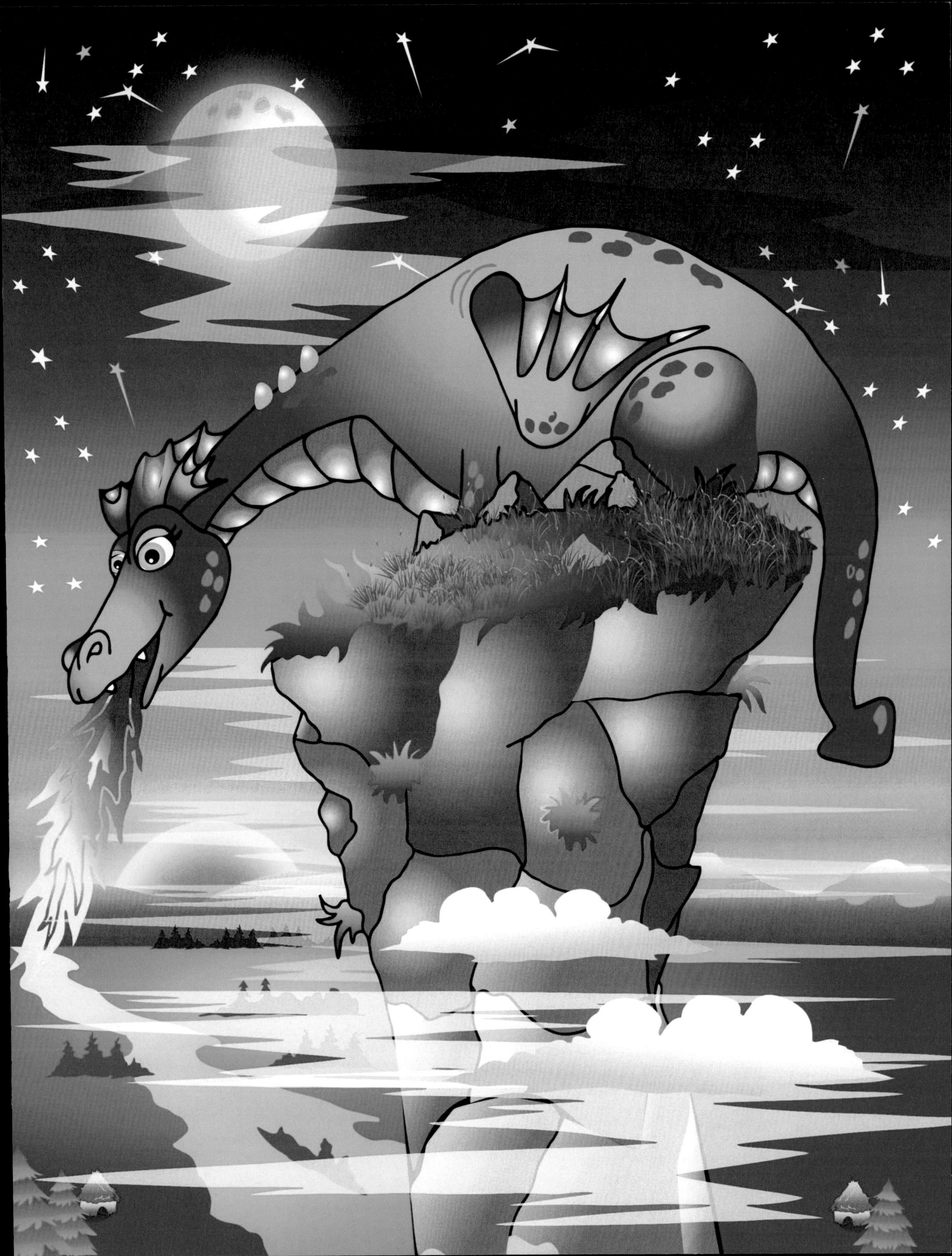

A dragon's heart has magical powers

That helps him rest on castle towers

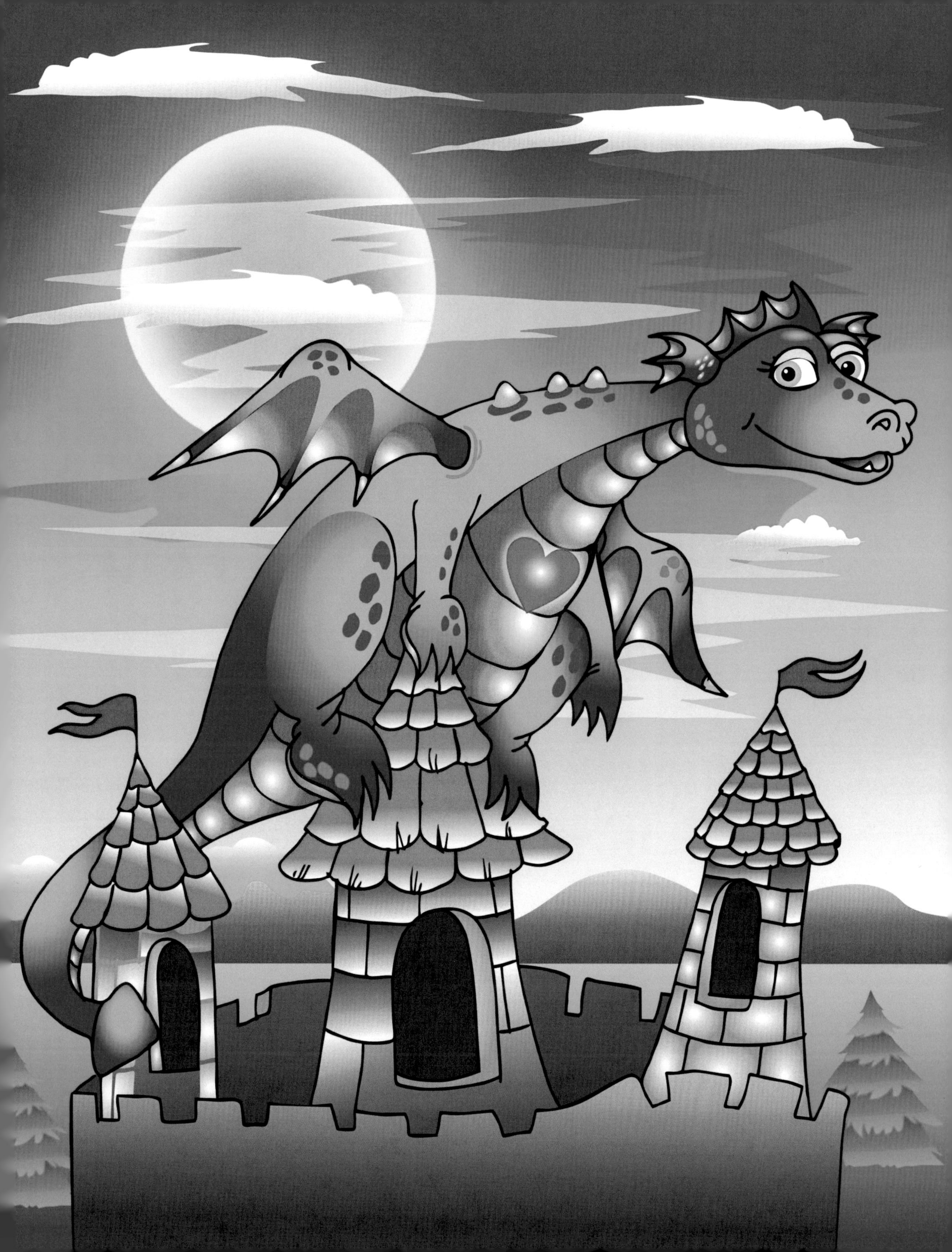

Dragons are seen in all sizes and kinds

But you must learn that they are hard to find

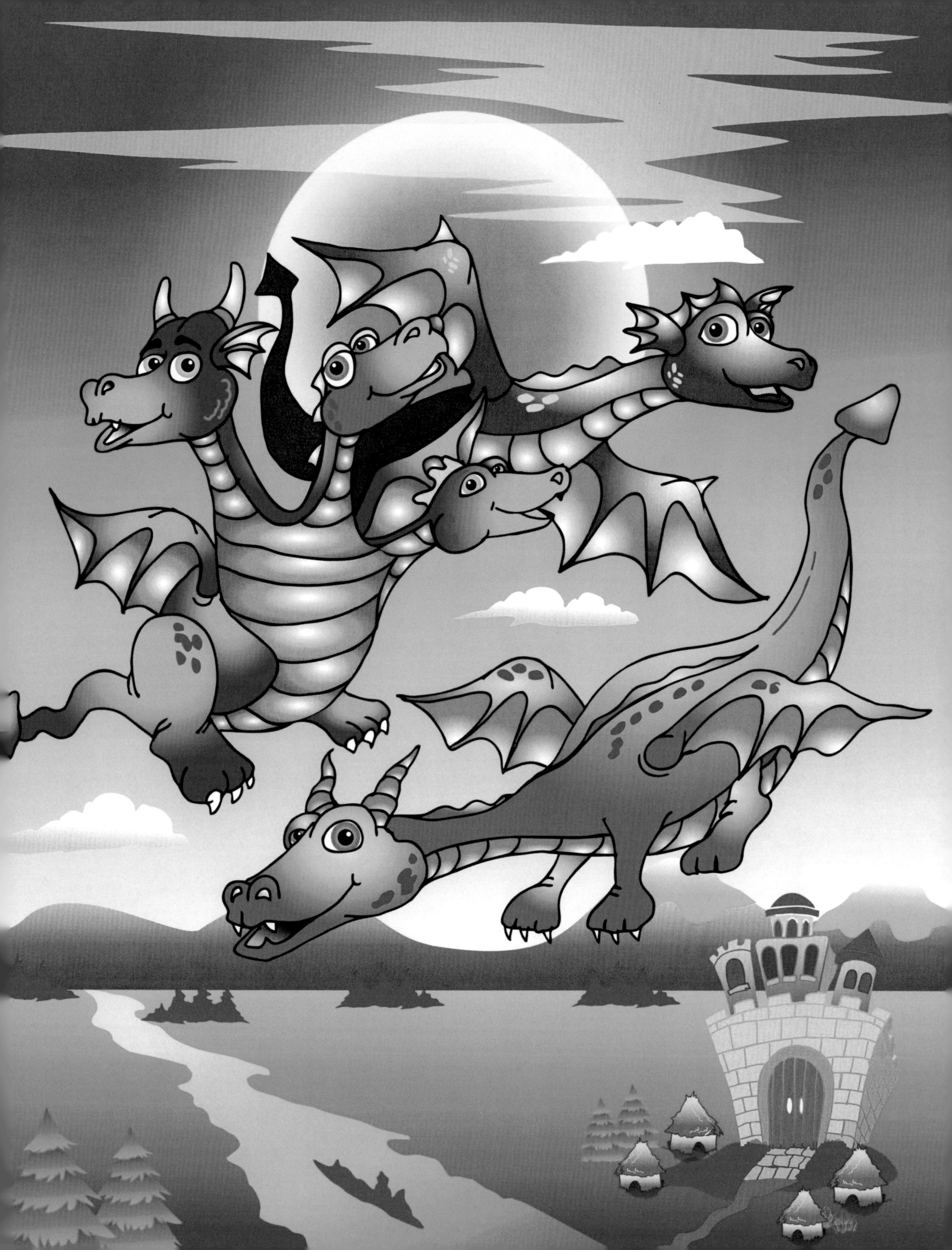

Dragons come in so many colors like red, black, and blue

But the best color of all is the color chosen by you

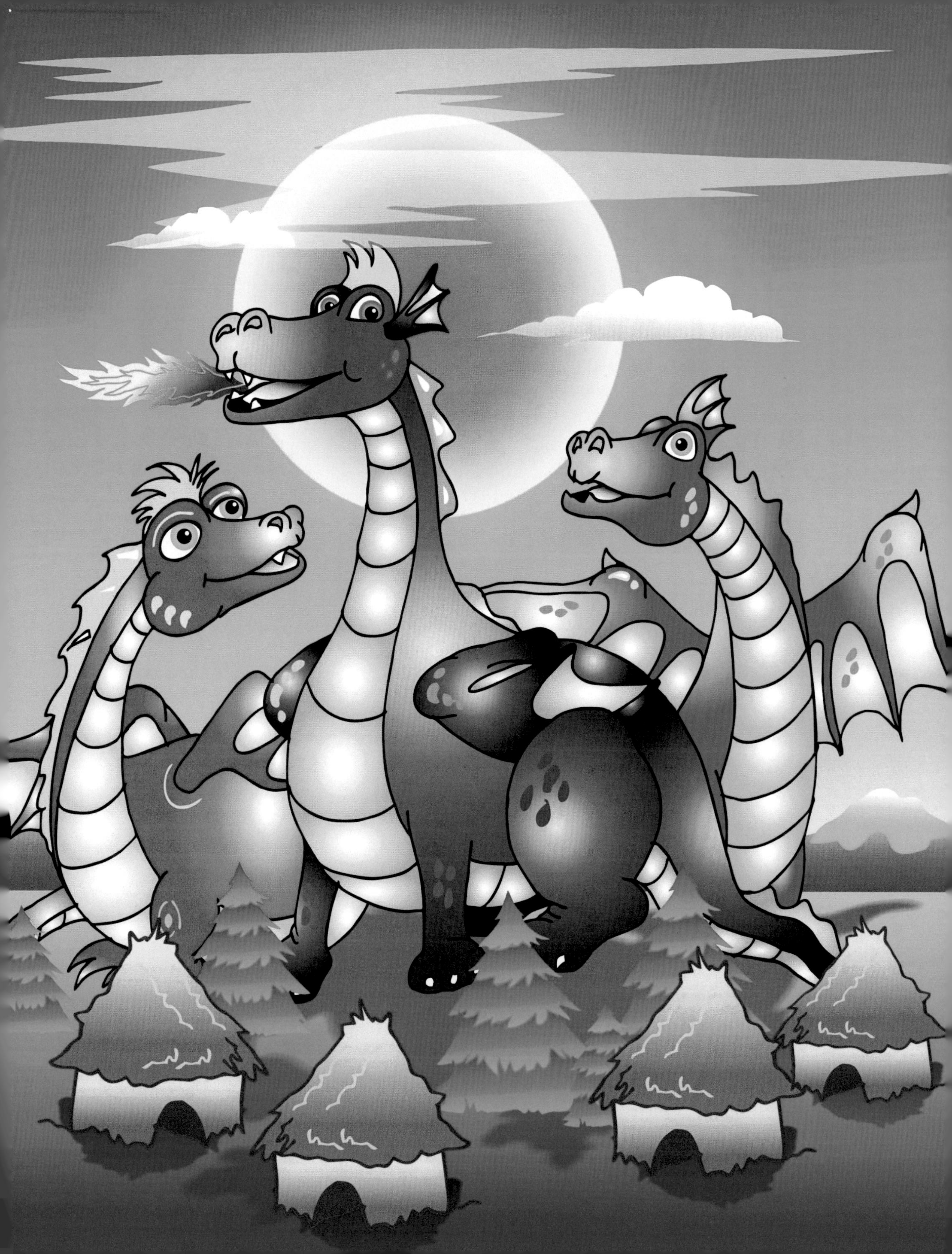

A dragon can see with powerful eyes

And they can see you when there high up in the sky

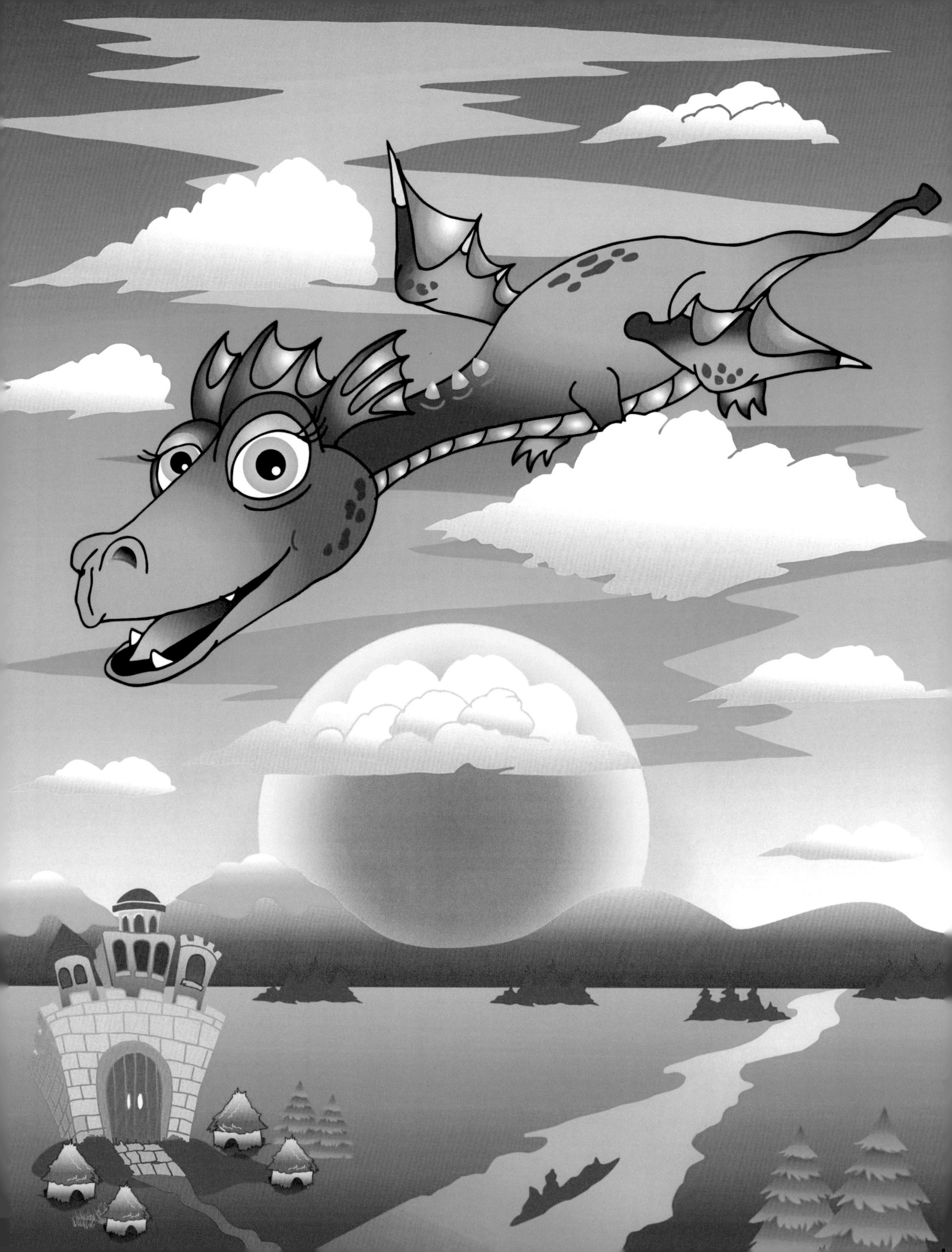

you must be strong and very brave

When you meet a dragon in it's cave

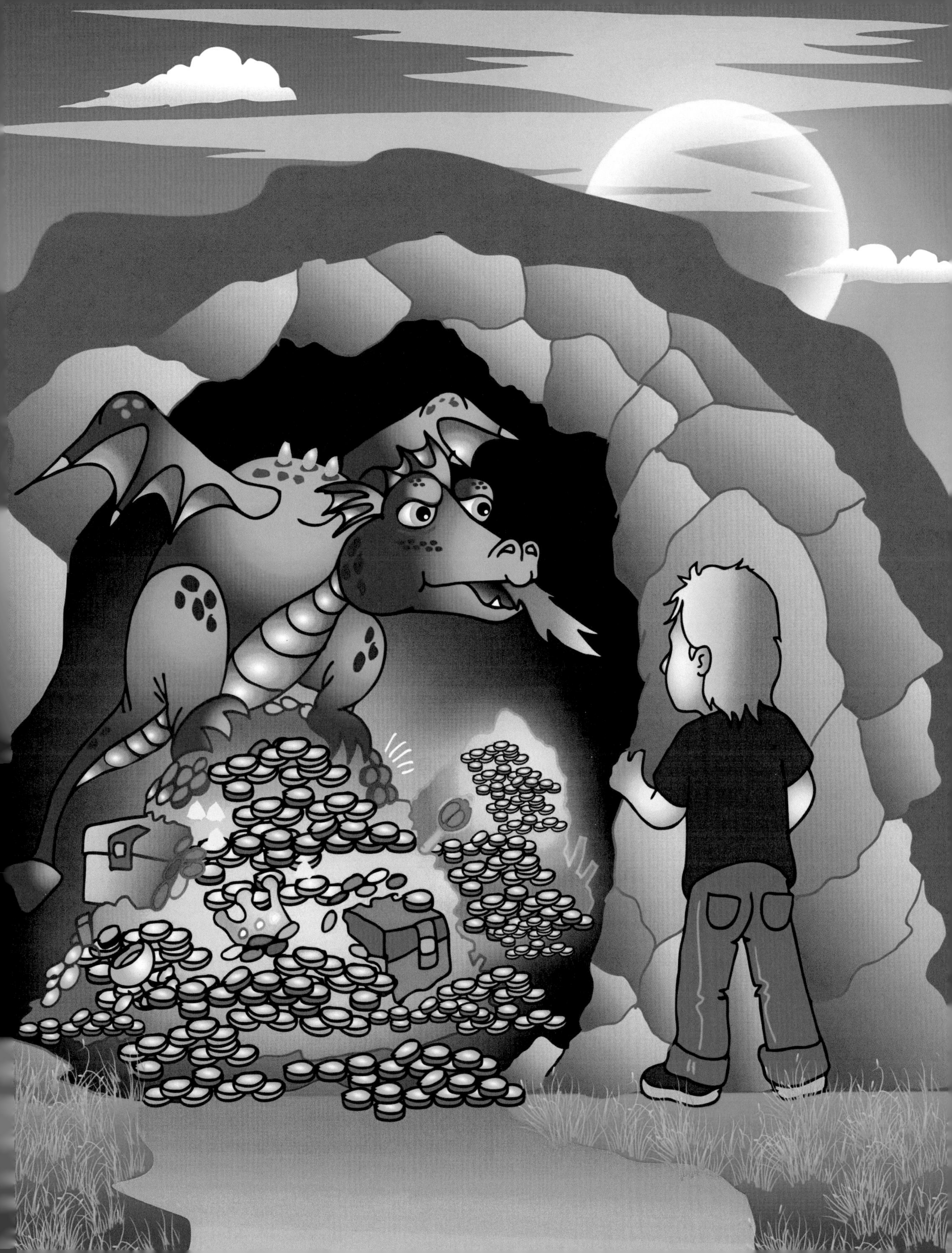

A momma dragon Loves her babies so much

Baby dragons Love to feel their mommas touch

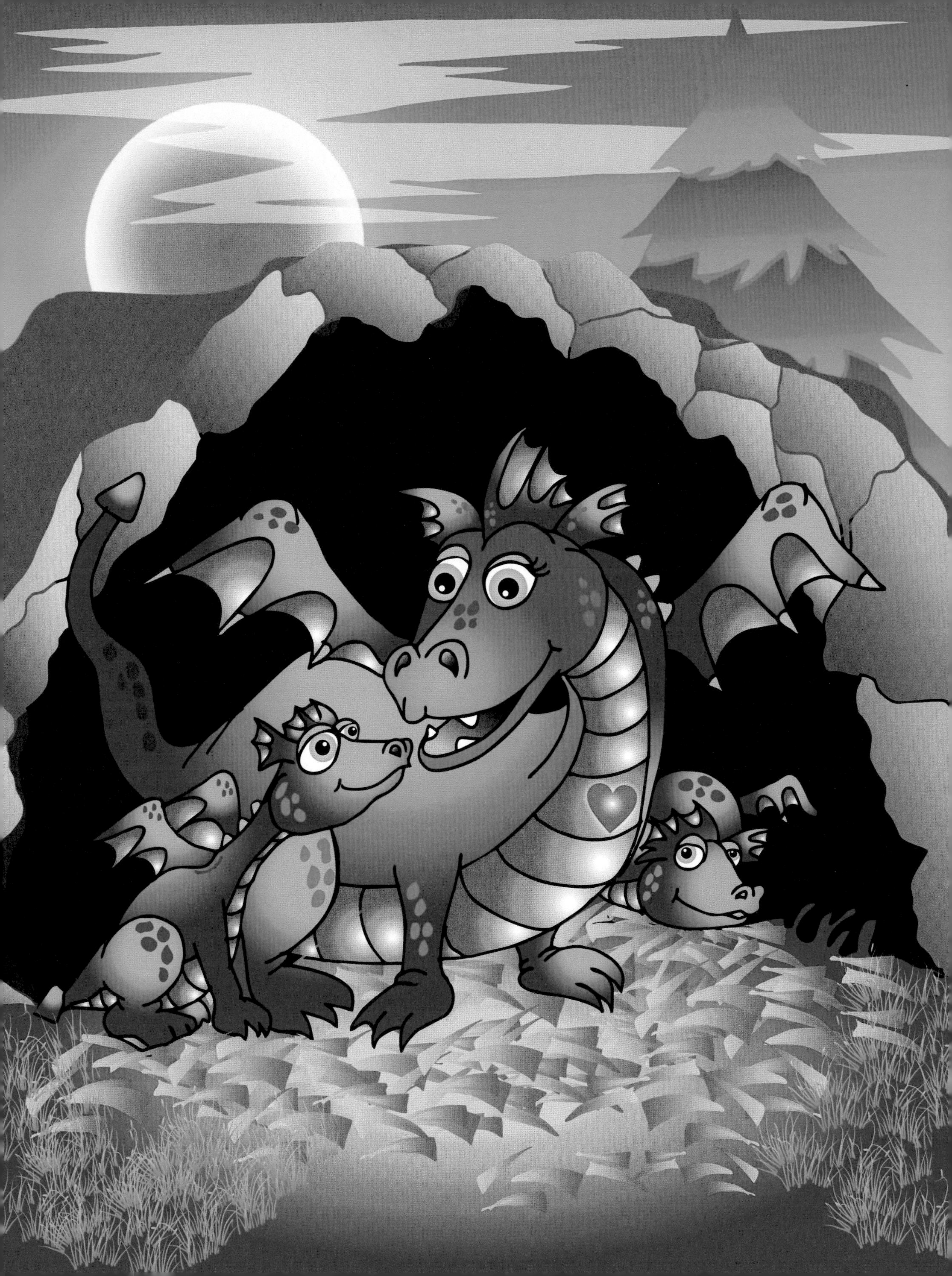

If you love a dragon
with all of your heart

You can learn all their
magic right from
the start

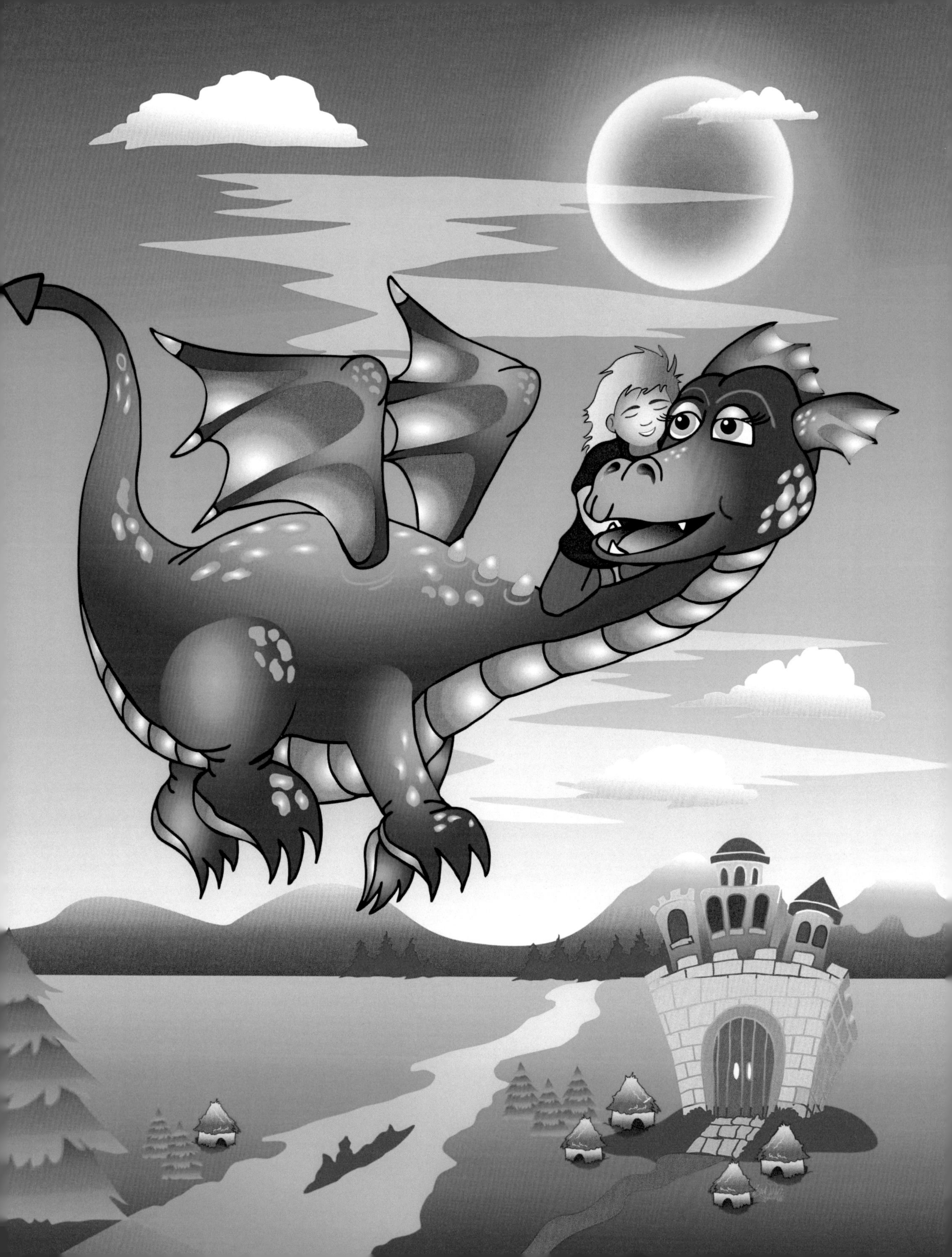

A dragon needs to know that you come as a friend

Because a dragon's friendship will never end

The End

color Me

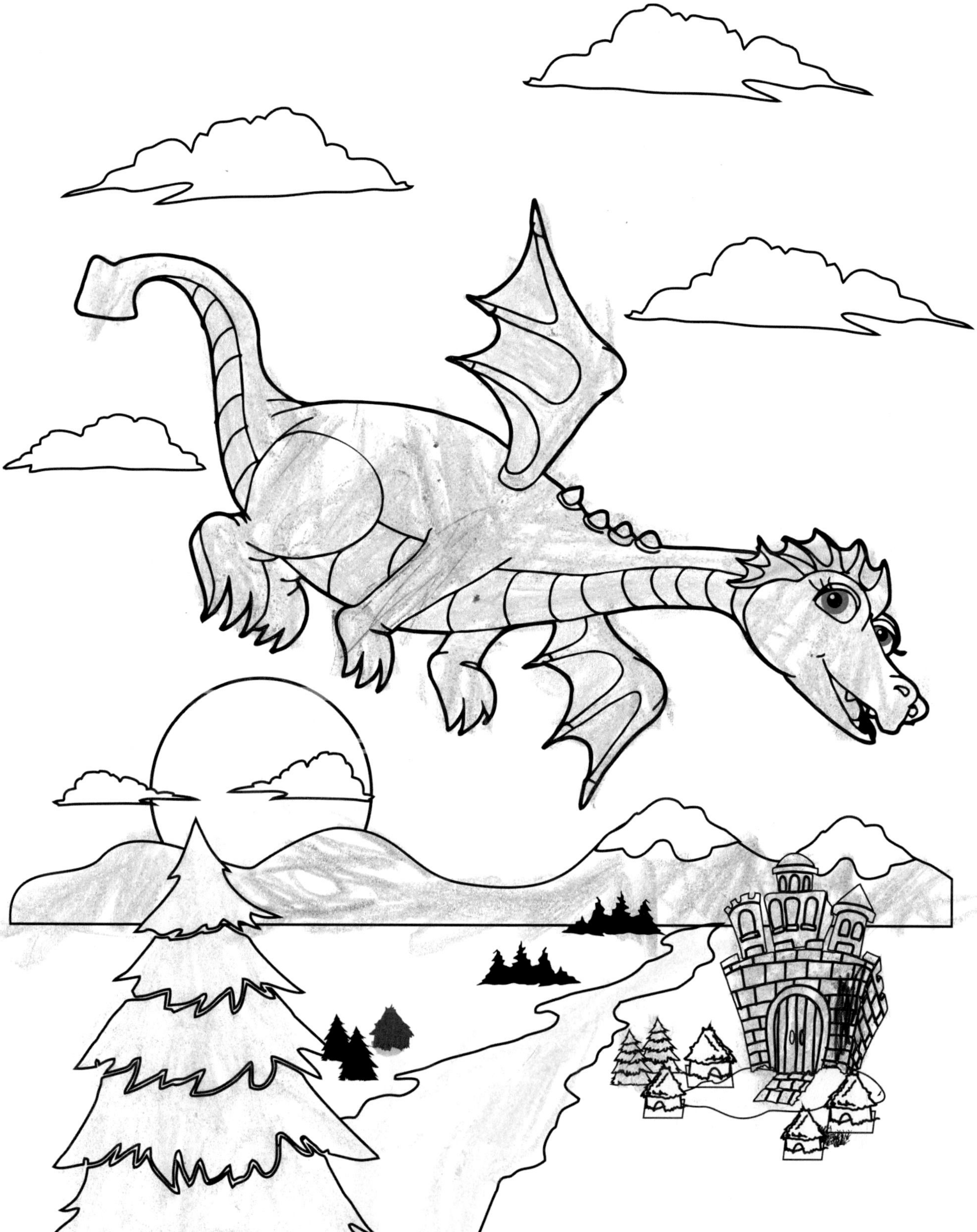

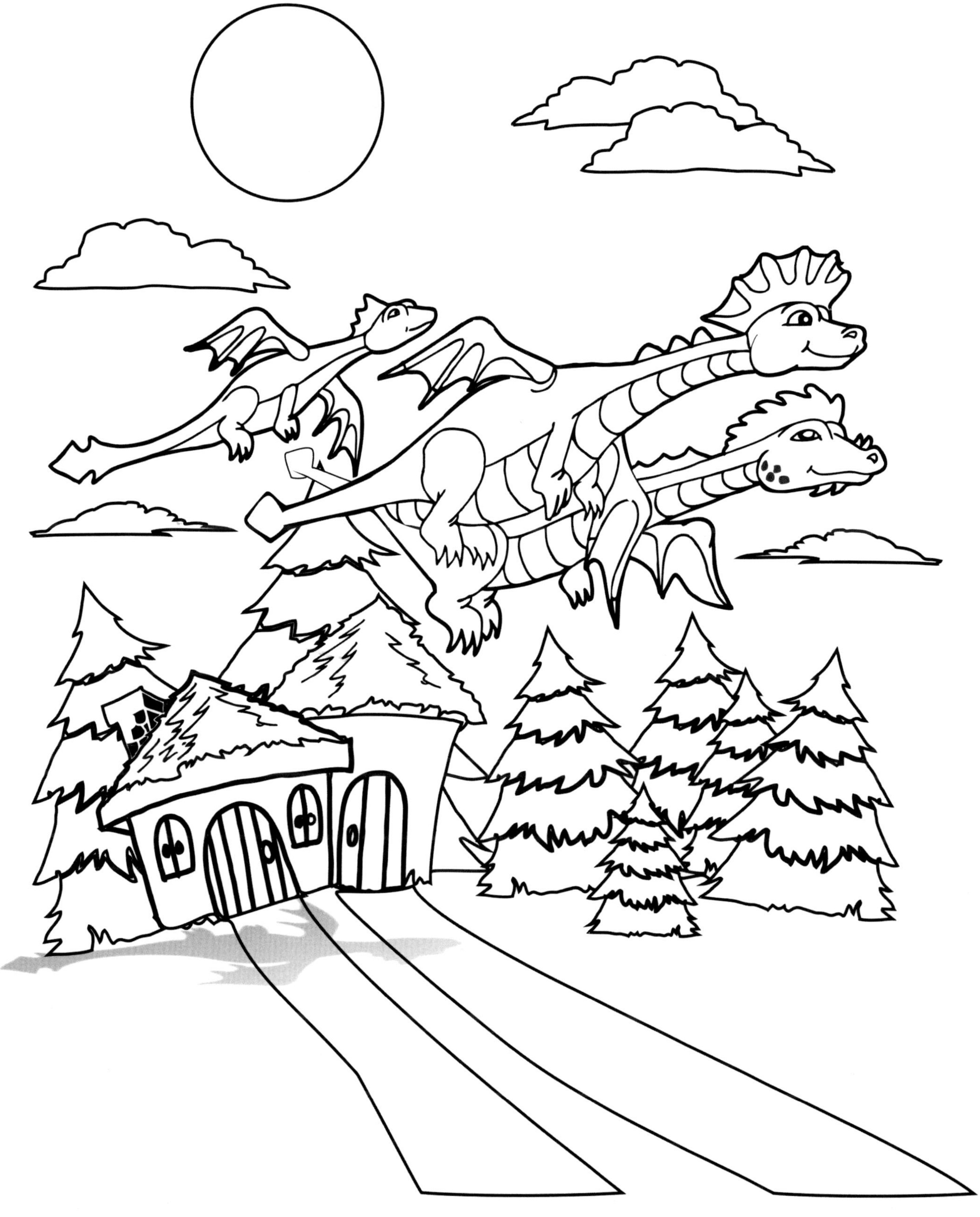

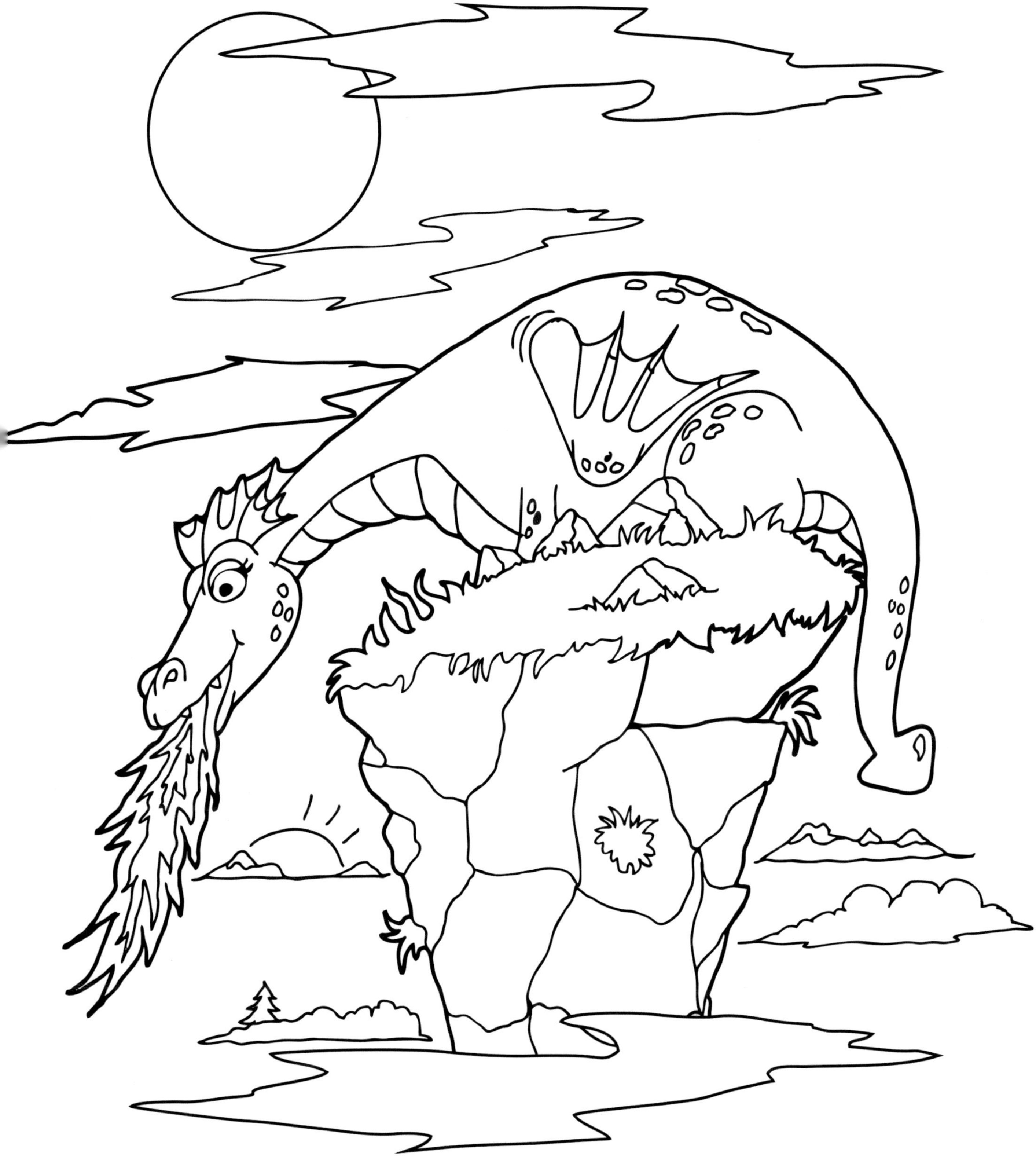

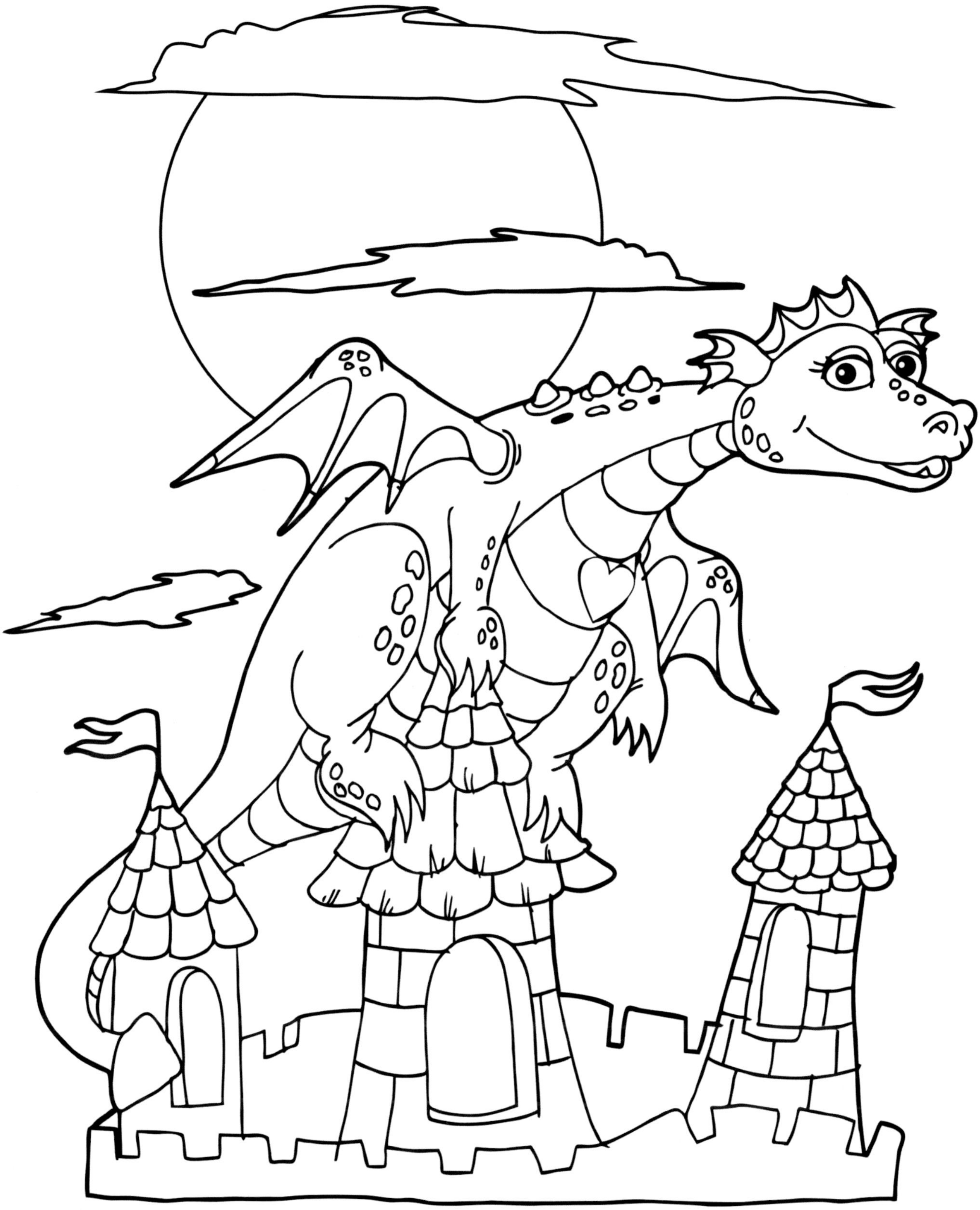

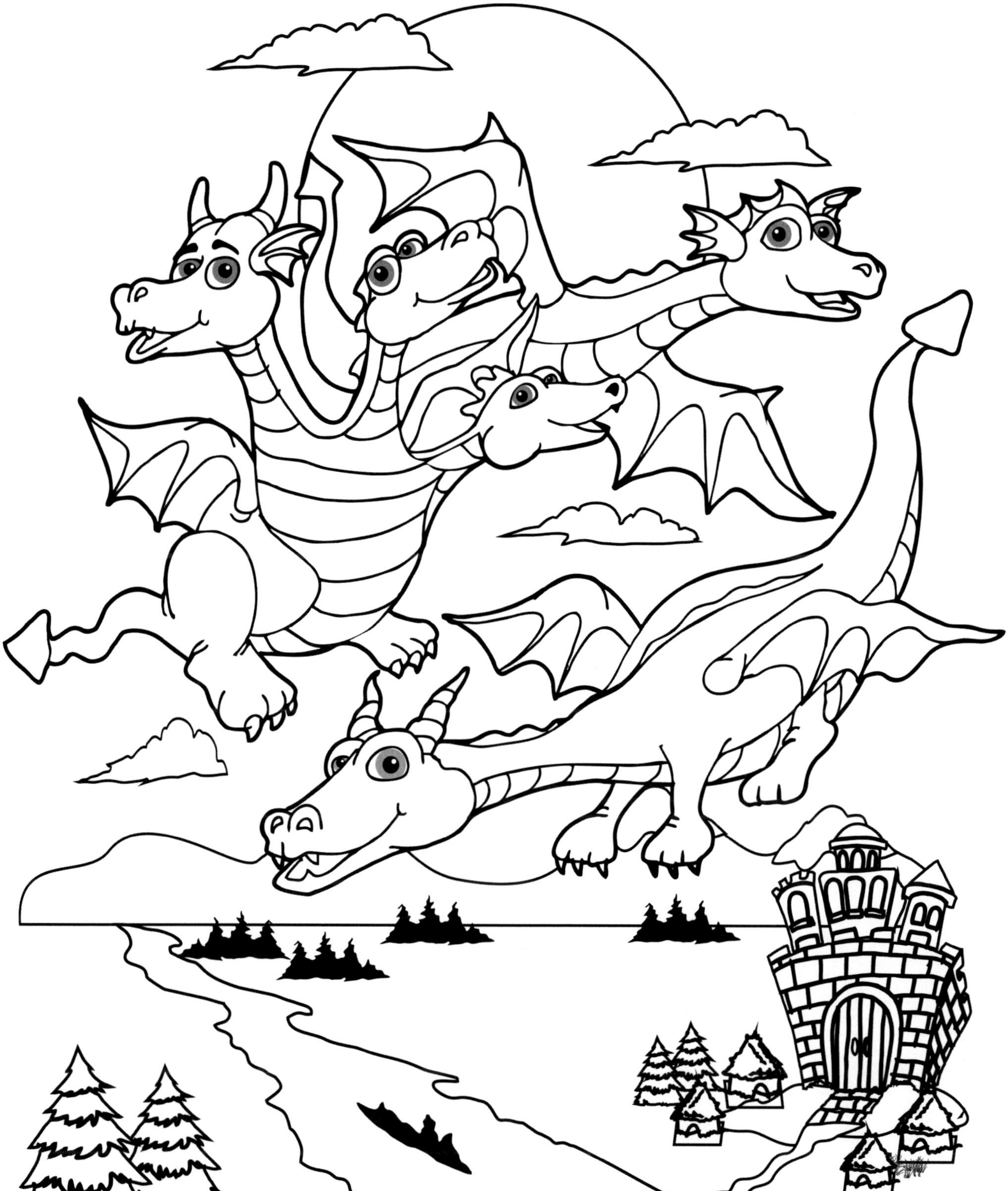

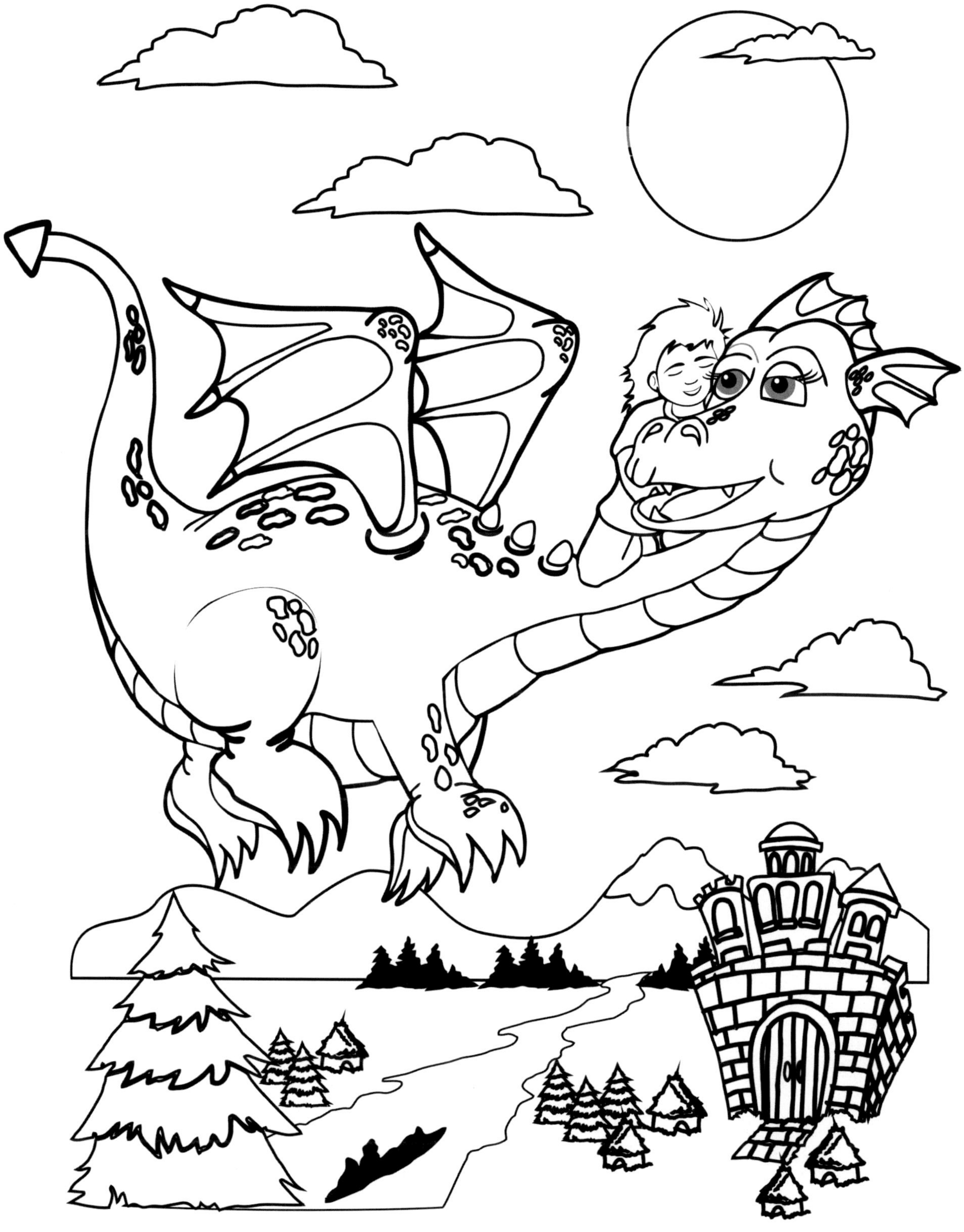

Made in the USA
San Bernardino, CA
28 June 2017